Created and Written by Romoulous Malachi
Illustration by Ivan Aguilar, David Reyes and AIU Comics
Production Design by Valtressa Washington

Published by MIROGLYPHICS
Library of Congress, Washington, D.C
Philadelphia, PA U.S.A.
ISBN-13: 978-0980107395
ISBN-10: 0980107393

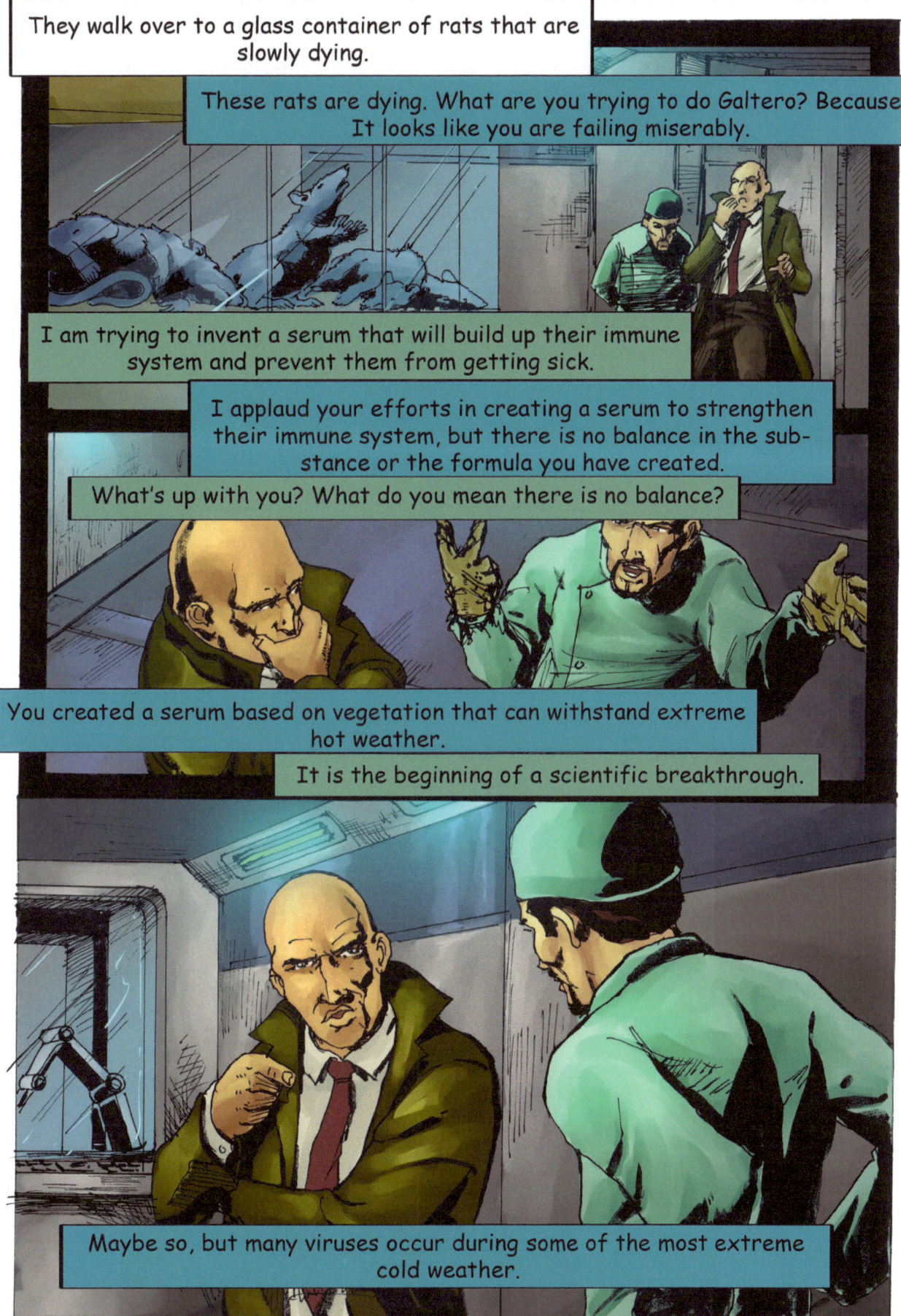

Maybe so, but many viruses occur during some of the most extreme cold weather.

Like the Flu virus, it remains more stable in cold, dry air than it does in high humidity environments, scientists have found.

The cold air pulls moisture out from the respiratory droplets propelled into the air by coughs and sneezes from infected individuals.

Because the viruses linger in the air for someone else to inhale.

Now we need to use two house plants that reflect the dominant influence of extreme cold weather.

And what plants do you have in mind?

Tundra Mosses are dominant vegetation at the North Pole and Microorganisms from South Pole.

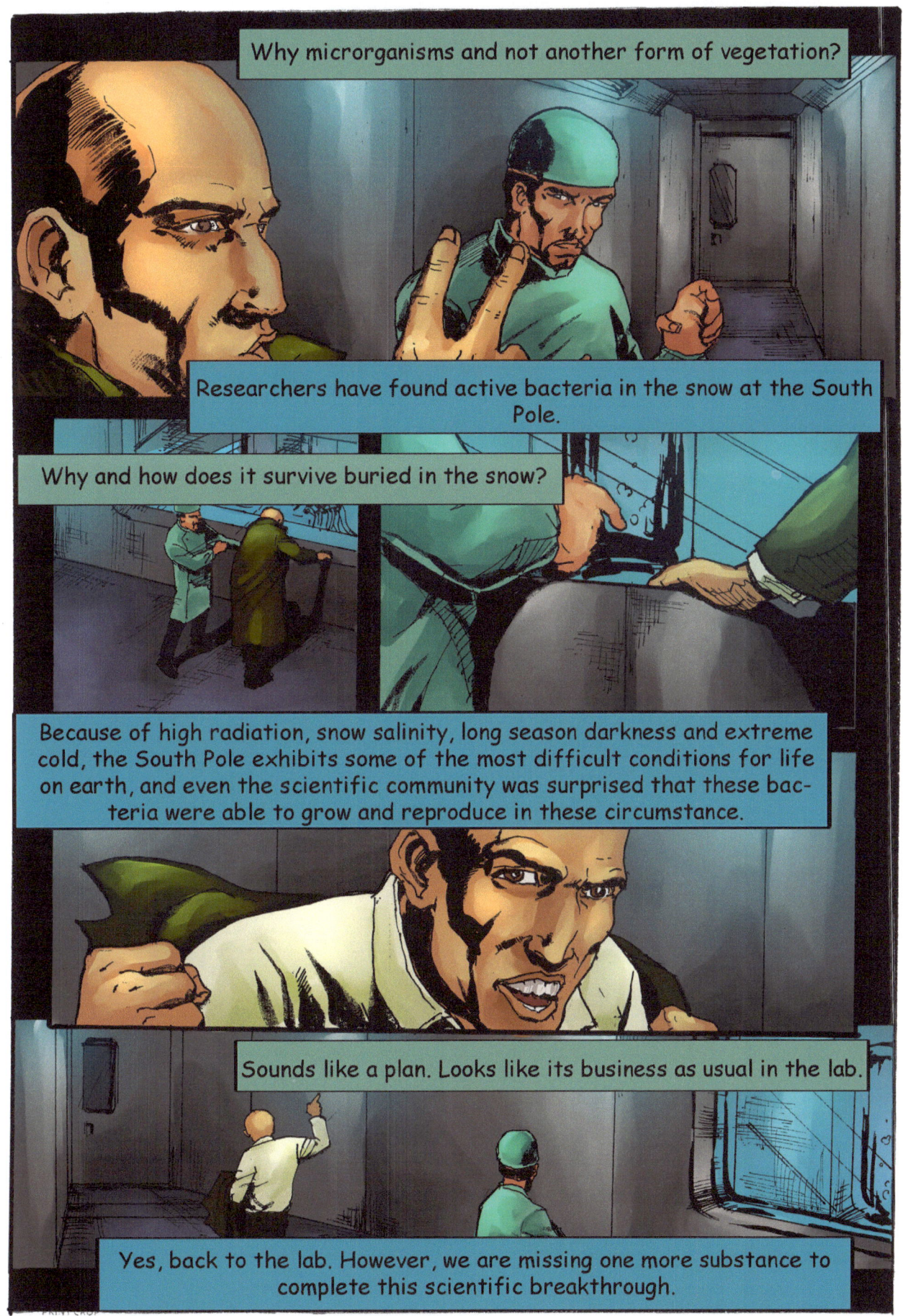

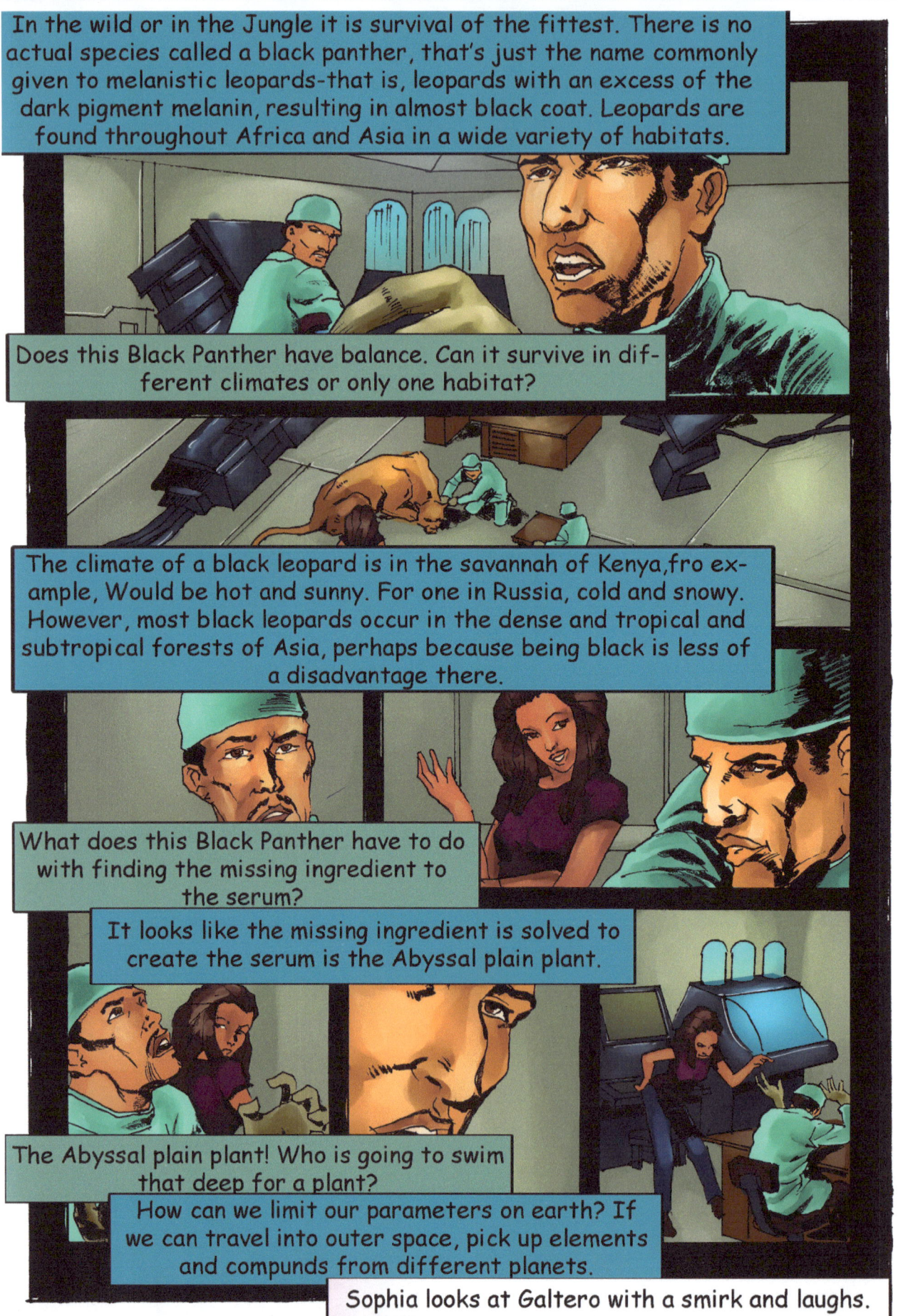

In the wild or in the Jungle it is survival of the fittest. There is no actual species called a black panther, that's just the name commonly given to melanistic leopards-that is, leopards with an excess of the dark pigment melanin, resulting in almost black coat. Leopards are found throughout Africa and Asia in a wide variety of habitats.

Does this Black Panther have balance. Can it survive in different climates or only one habitat?

The climate of a black leopard is in the savannah of Kenya,fro example, Would be hot and sunny. For one in Russia, cold and snowy. However, most black leopards occur in the dense and tropical and subtropical forests of Asia, perhaps because being black is less of a disadvantage there.

What does this Black Panther have to do with finding the missing ingredient to the serum?

It looks like the missing ingredient is solved to create the serum is the Abyssal plain plant.

The Abyssal plain plant! Who is going to swim that deep for a plant?

How can we limit our parameters on earth? If we can travel into outer space, pick up elements and compunds from different planets.

Sophia looks at Galtero with a smirk and laughs.

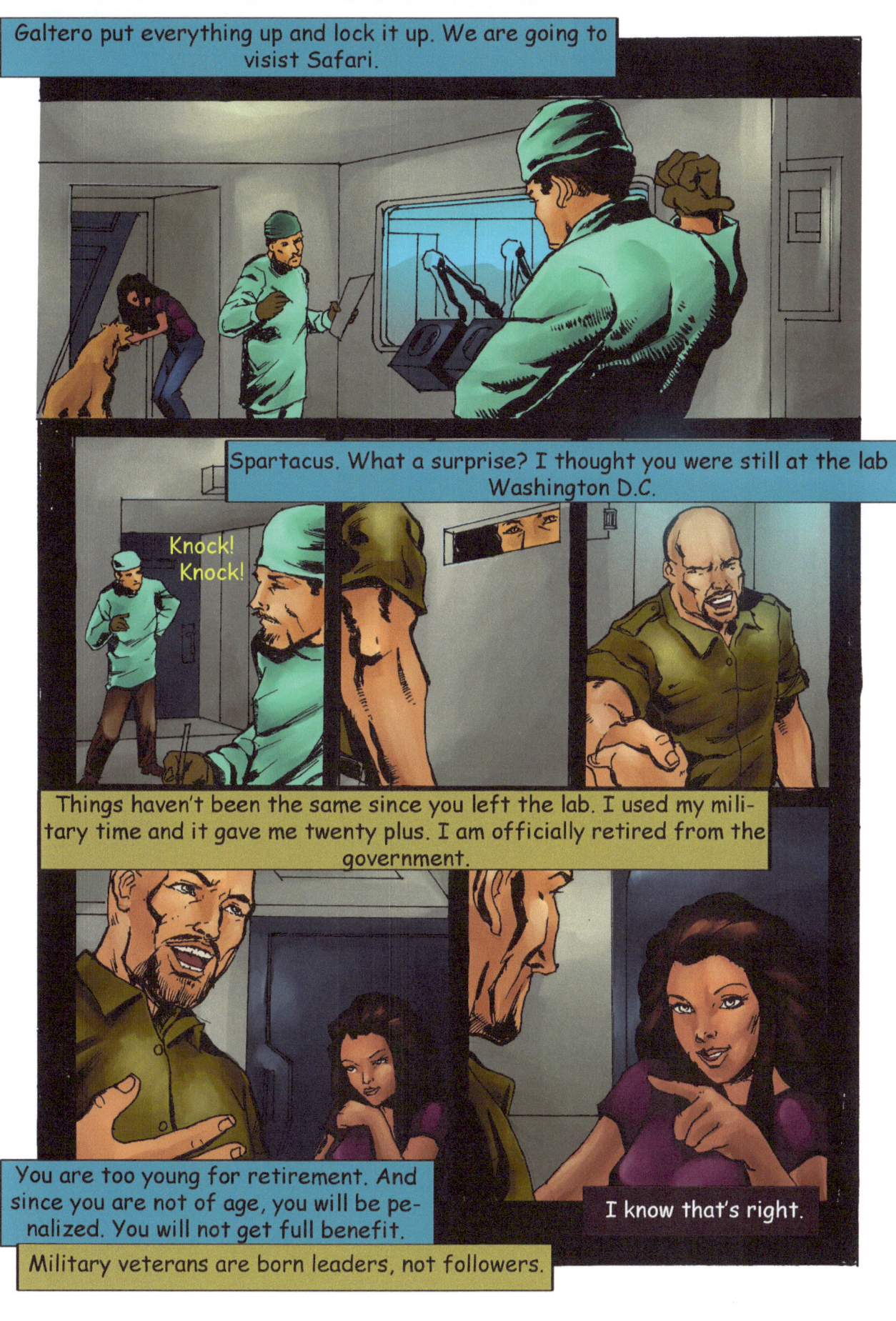

Dr. safari, I apologize for the interruptions. I can assure you that Galtero will not cause anymore disturbances. Especially when a transfer can take place to another department at the Bronze Zoo anytime. Isn't that right Galtero?

Galtero recognizes that Dr. Ziegler means business and becomes silent.

Titanium is the perfect blend of strength and practicality. It's low density makes it perfect for industrial work that uses a strong metal with a high melting point.

Indeed, Titanium has the highest strength to weight ratio of any metal known to man. Pure Titanium is stronger than standard steel, while being less than half the weight, and can be made into even stronger alloys.

Because it is also fairly common, it's no wonder Titanium is used for a multitude of purposes. When it comes to manufacturing, the only strong, natural metal worth caring for is this.

You also have twenty-three other elements on display.

Allanite is a sorosilicate group of minerals within the epidote group that contains a significant amount of rare earth elements. The mineral occurs mainly in metamorphosed clay rich sediments and felsic igneous rocks.

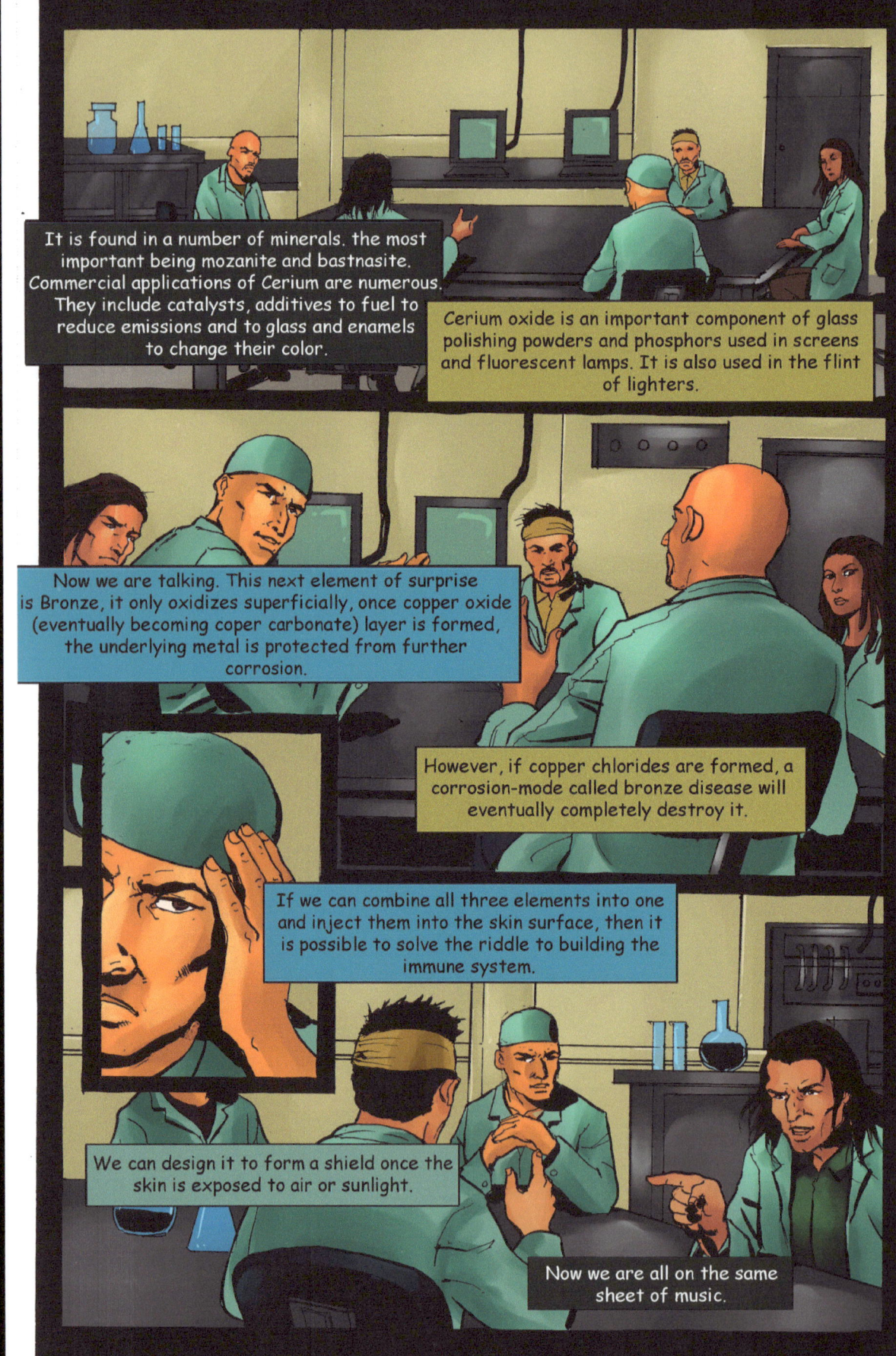

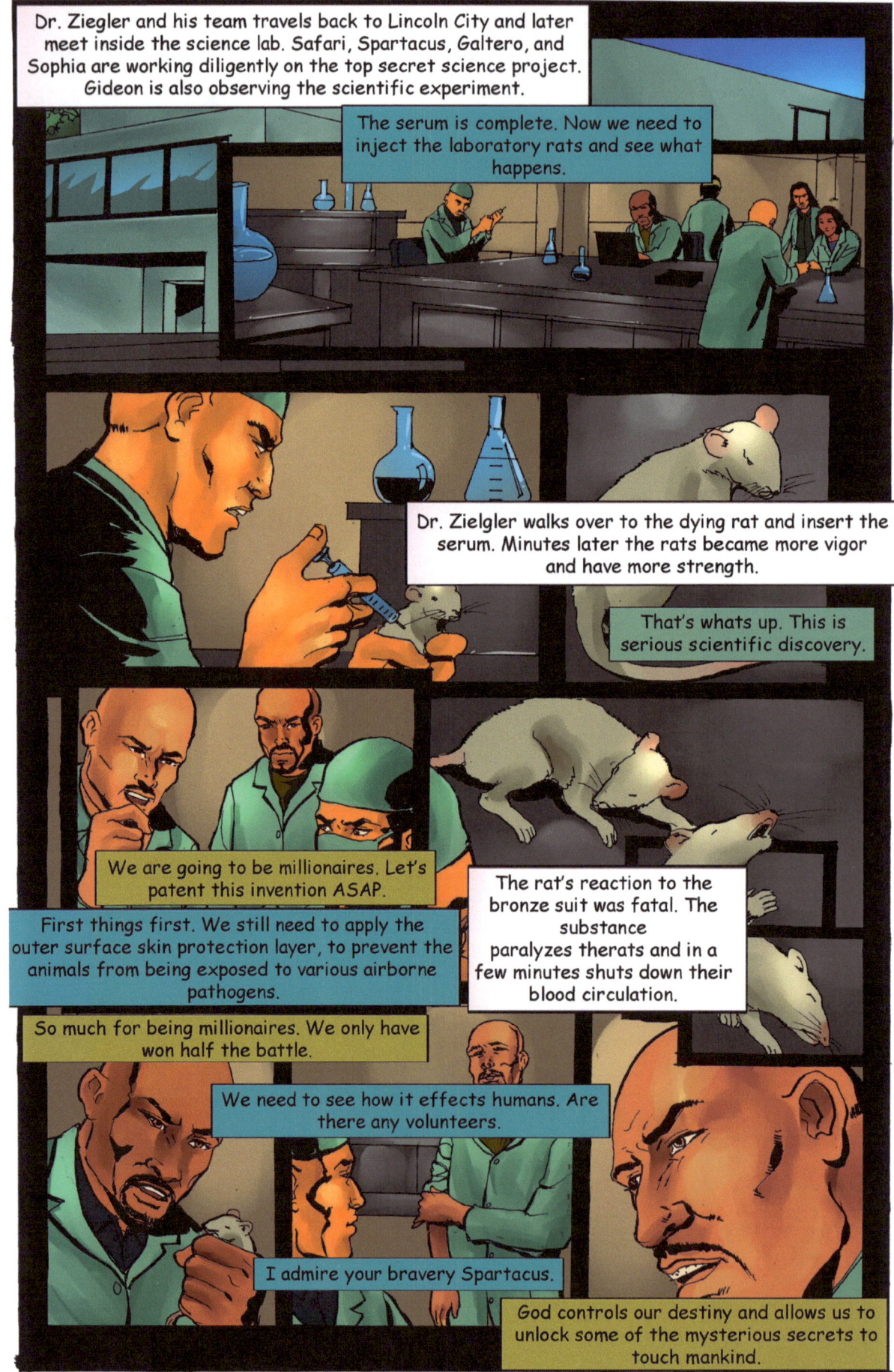

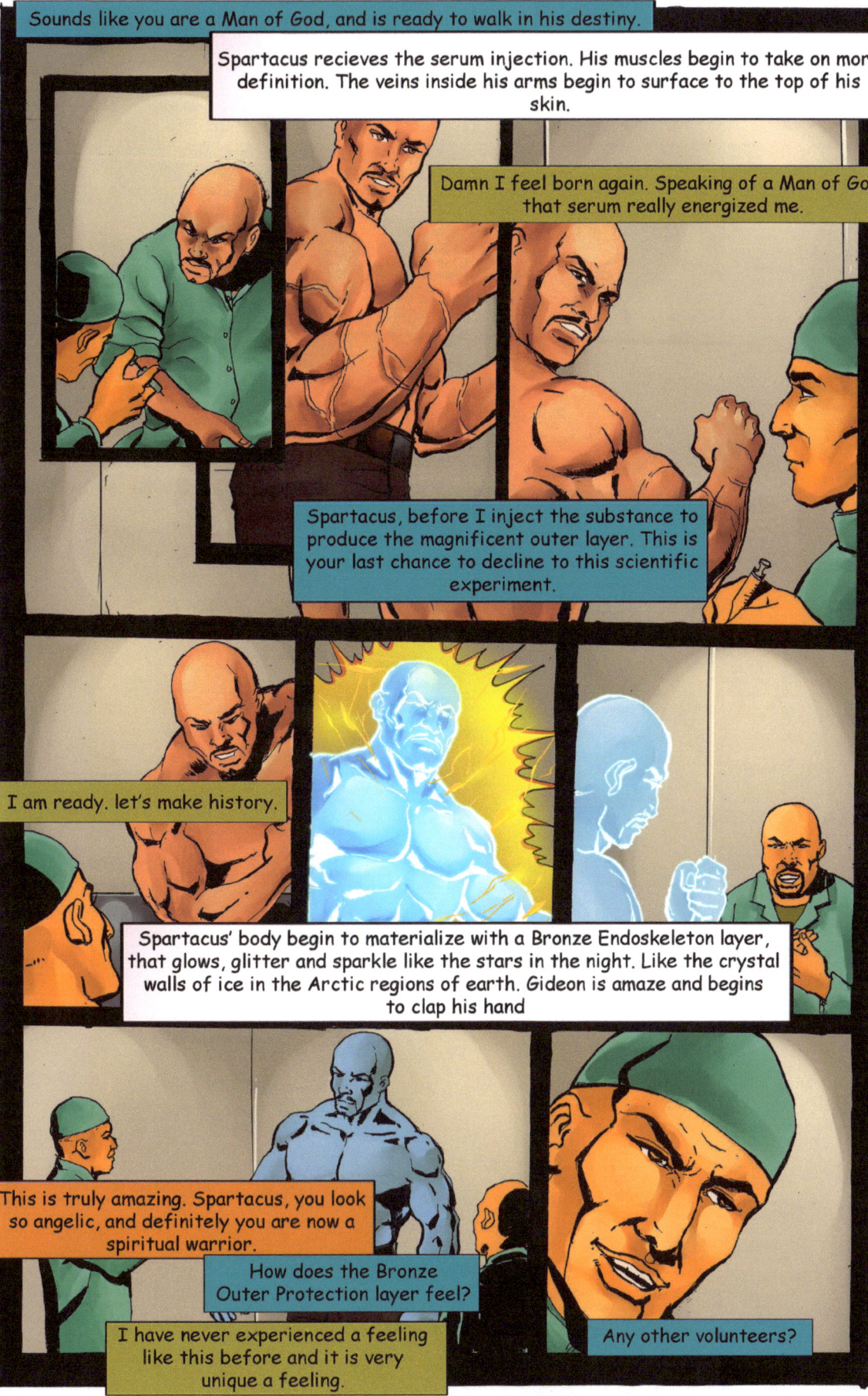

Ramona has two guest passes to enter the facility. She also has an access card to enter inside Dr.Ziegler's lab.

At the Bronze Zoo, there is an African-American man patrolling the area, named Lexus. He is a veteran of the United States Marines, and also the head security at the zoo along with three other security guards, who are marines at a local reserve unit in Lincoln City. Their names are Cosmo, who comes from Vietnam, Batari from Indonesia and Kaapo who is from Saudi Arabia.

Lexus recognizes Ramona and walks over to greet her.

Ramona, what a pleasant surprise. What brings you here at the Bronze Zoo?

Hey Lexus, I'm here with my brother Malachi to see our father.

Dr.Ziegler and his team went out to lunch. They should be arriving shortly.

Very well, just tell my dad we will come back later today.

No problem. Me an Malachi will wait for him inside the lab.

Unfortunataley, Dr. ziegler has given us orders to monitor and provide security until they return back to the lab.

Not at all, we can escort you and Malachi inside the lab until he returns.

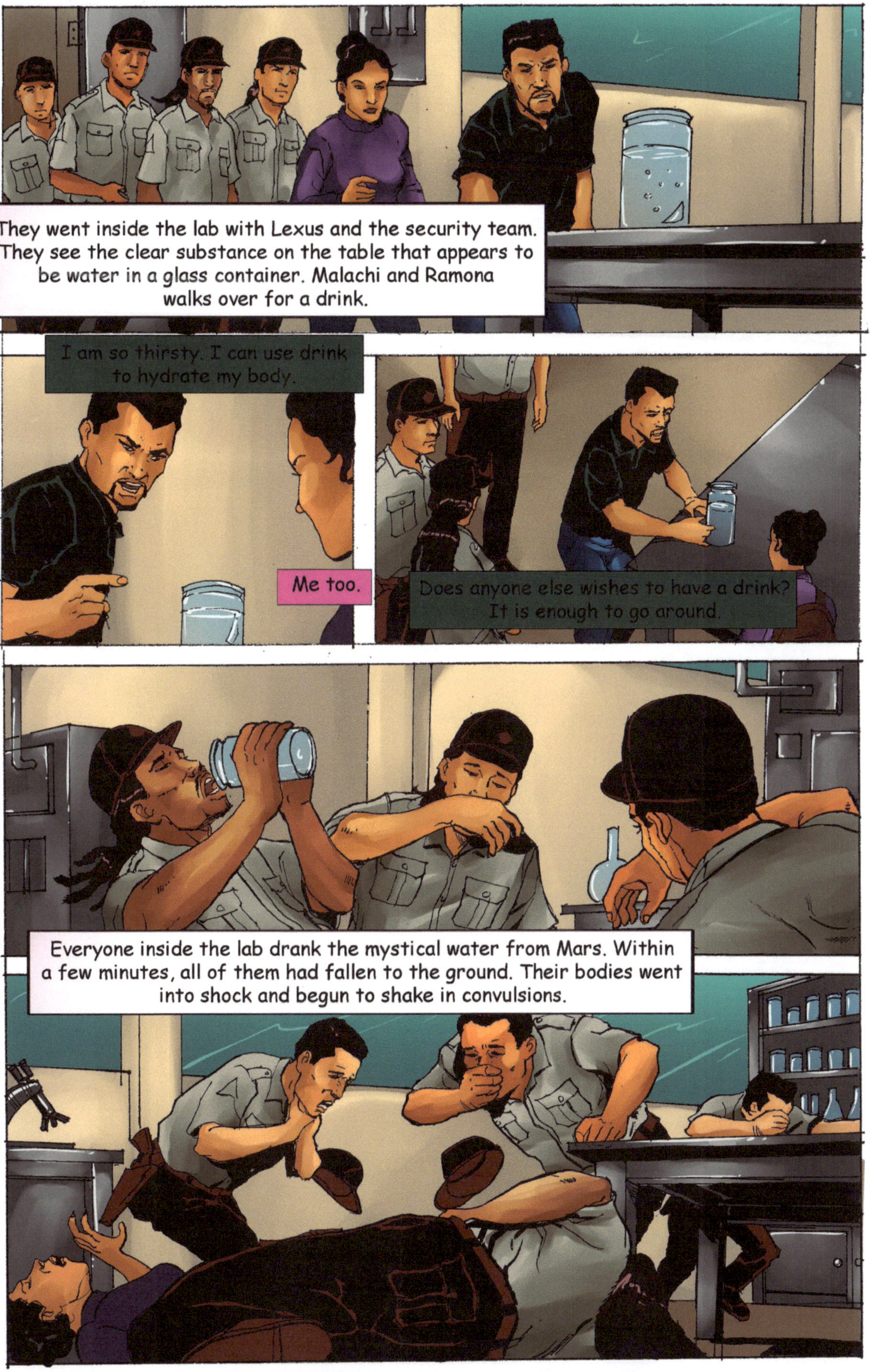

They went inside the lab with Lexus and the security team. They see the clear substance on the table that appears to be water in a glass container. Malachi and Ramona walks over for a drink.

I am so thirsty. I can use drink to hydrate my body.

Me too.

Does anyone else wishes to have a drink? It is enough to go around.

Everyone inside the lab drank the mystical water from Mars. Within a few minutes, all of them had fallen to the ground. Their bodies went into shock and begun to shake in convulsions.

What the hell
is inside this water?
Maybe we should have asked before
assuming. This is a science lab.
I feel something moving inside me, and
it feels like Im catching the Holy Ghost.

Malachi is the first one to experience the metamorphic change in his body.
His body turned extremely hot and ripped his shirt. His hives begins to increase in 3
three to four inches in width. Then his back and shoulder pushes out metal spikes with
a height ranging five to six inches. Ramona and the others look in total amazement.
Then she became afraid of what had become of her brother.

Malachi! there is something
in that water that we drank.

Are you serious! Look at me! It has turned me
into a freak! As twisted as this may sound.
No more hives!

Then suddenly Ramona and the others begin to experience a spontaneous reaction. Ramona's back begins to open and develops razor sharp wings.

Then she suddenly flies inside the lab as her new wings guide her around the lab.

Then she manages to take control and lowers herself down to the surface of the floor.

When you ran the track and did the long jump. Everybody always said that you have hidden wings. Yes, there is something in this water.

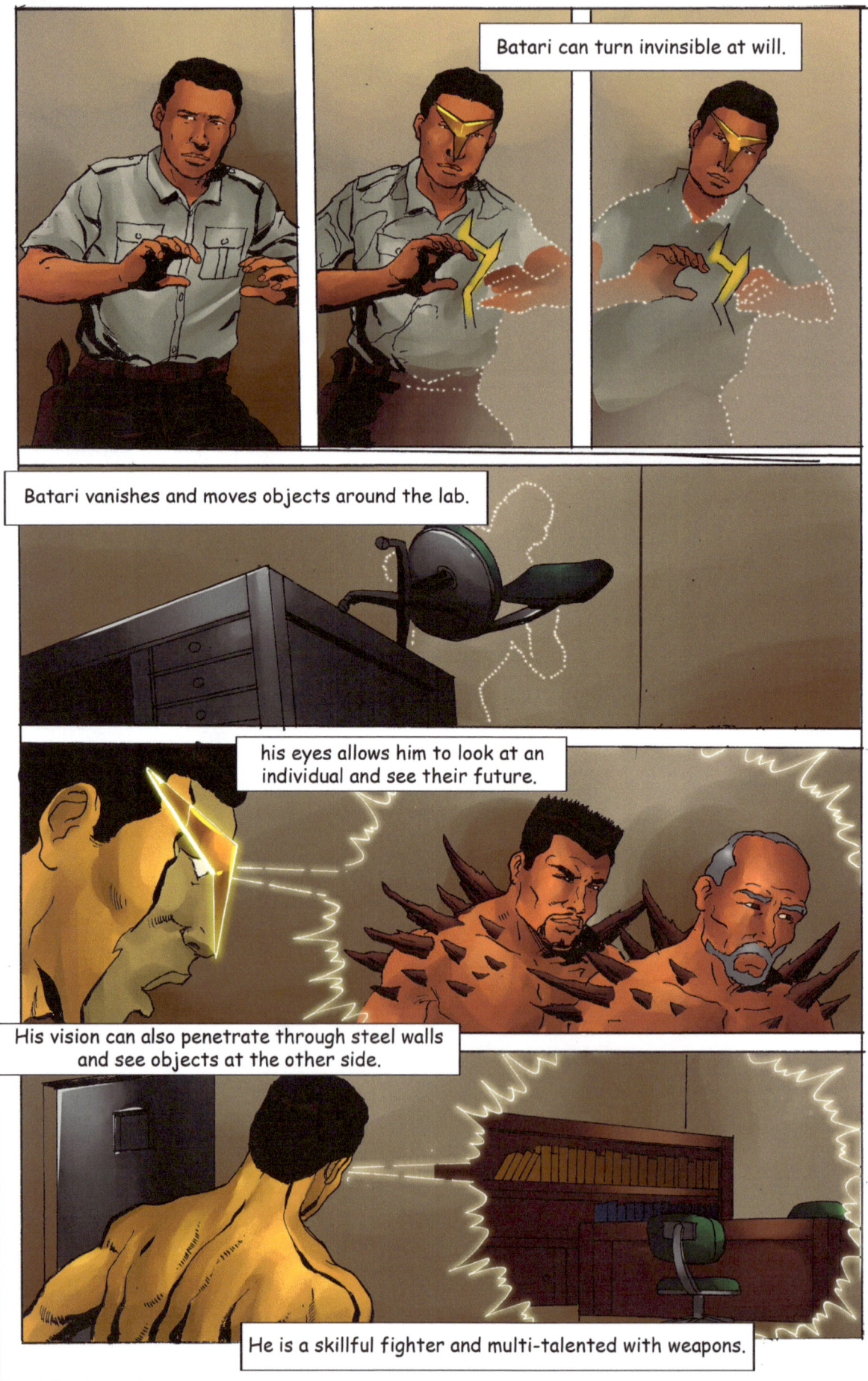

Everyone is astonished inside the lab and was silently contemplating about their new powers.

Until suddenly Dr. Ziegler and his scientists came back froim their lunch.

Safari looks at the table and sees the liquid substance from Mars is no longer on display. He becomes furious and demanded some answers.

Where is my liquid substance? What the hell are you guys doing here? Who authorized this! I want answers now!

Lexus was unaware that inside the serum was also the liquid substance that Dr. Ziegler and his team of scientists have had already taken.

Their special powers are more contolled because of the other biological component added with the liquid substance.

Lexus opened his hands ready to charge at Dr. Ziegler but unbeknownst to him the doctor already knew what was going to transpire before entering the lab.

The doctor creates a magnetic shield that reverse Lexus' electric charge and it knocks Lexus along with his security team.

Oh no! My children are now supernatural genetic freaks.

Safari injects both Malachi and Ramona with the serum.

It looks we also have two new members on our team.

What kind of madness is this? You did a scientific experiment on rats!

These are some of the lowest form of rodents and are very disgusting.

Even the lowest form of life deserve an opportunity to help build an empire.

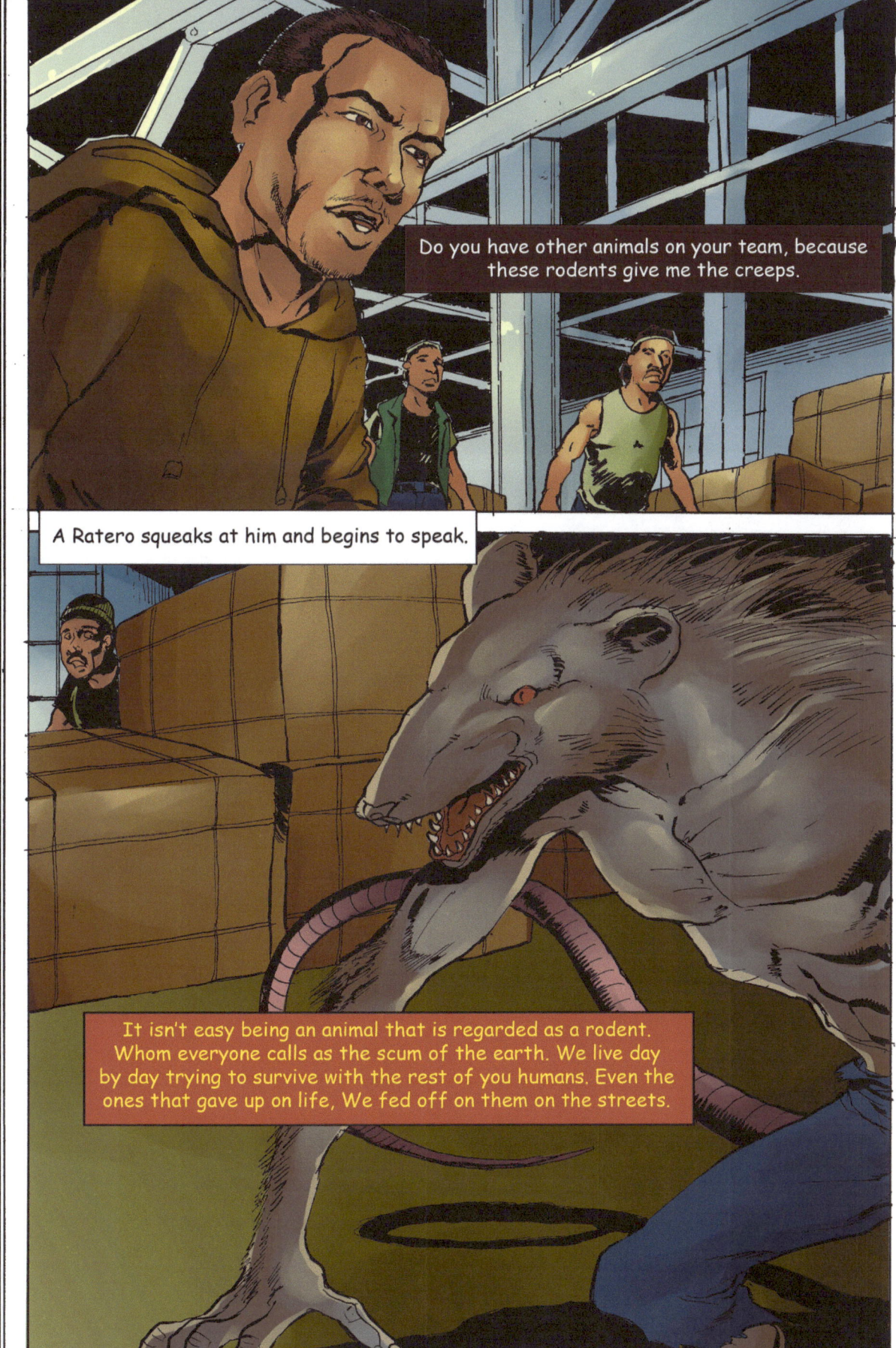

Do you have other animals on your team, because these rodents give me the creeps.

A Ratero squeaks at him and begins to speak.

It isn't easy being an animal that is regarded as a rodent. Whom everyone calls as the scum of the earth. We live day by day trying to survive with the rest of you humans. Even the ones that gave up on life, We fed off on them on the streets.

# COMING SOON:
# KATALAMBANO

www.ingramcontent.com/pod-product-compliance
Lightning Source LLC
Chambersburg PA
CBHW041538240626

47164CB00002B/49